Little Sister

Karen's Candy
Ann M. Martin

Illustrations by Susan Tang

A
LITTLE APPLE
PAPERBACK

SCHOLASTIC INC.
New York Toronto London Auckland Sydney

ISBN 0-590-48301-3

12 11 10 9 8 7 6 5 4 3 2 1   4 5 6 7 8 9/9

Printed in the U.S.A.   40

First Scholastic printing, October 1994

*In honor of the birth of
Rebecca Mary Bowen Goodman*

Karen's Candy

**Look for these
and other books about Karen
in the
Baby-sitters Little Sister series:**

Karen's Candy

Autumn

"Karen," said Nancy Dawes, "you know what you should be for Halloween this year? A turtle. Maybe Yertle the Turtle."

"A turtle? Why?" I asked.

Nancy shrugged.

"No, she should be Goldilocks, since she has blonde hair," said Hannie Papadakis.

Nancy and Hannie are my two best friends. I am Karen Brewer. I do have blonde hair (also blue eyes and some freckles), but I did not want to be Goldilocks for Halloween. Still, I was glad my friends

1

wanted to help me think of a Halloween costume. That is what good friends do. They help each other. Nancy and Hannie and I are such good friends that we call ourselves the Three Musketeers. We are seven years old, and we are all in Ms. Colman's second-grade class at Stoneybrook Academy here in Stoneybrook, Connecticut. We play together, we have sleepovers together, and we like each other and help each other.

On that autumn day we were sitting in Nancy's front yard. The leaves were falling around us, and I was feeling happy. To me, autumn means Halloween, and Halloween means other holidays are just around the corner. I love holidays.

Hannie held up a bright yellow leaf. "Let's make a leaf collection," she said. She reached for a red leaf and then an orange one.

I giggled. "The last time Seth said 'Let's make a leaf collection,' you know what he

meant? He meant he wanted us to rake the yard."

Hannie and Nancy laughed, too. And Nancy said, "That's sneaky."

I nodded. "Yeah. Seth can be sneaky, but he is funny, too."

Seth is my stepfather. He is married to Mommy, and he and Mommy live next door to Nancy. Daddy and my stepmother live in another neighborhood. They live across the street from Hannie. That means that my little brother Andrew and I have two homes. We live at both of them. We go back and forth, a month here, a month there. October was a month at Mommy's and Seth's house. I am glad my two houses are both in Stoneybrook, so the Three Musketeers can spend lots of time together.

"Nancy, maybe *you* could be Yertle the Turtle this year," I said.

"Maybe," replied Nancy. "I have to think about it."

"I want to be a Popsicle," spoke up Hannie.

4

"You do? Brrr," I said. I paused. Then I added, "Hey, I really am cold. It's getting chilly. Let's go inside."

"Okay, but not inside *my* house," said Nancy. "Danny is sleeping." (Danny is Nancy's baby brother. Nancy got to name him herself.)

"Let's go to my house then," I said.

So we did. And since we were cold, Mommy fixed hot chocolate for us.

She fixed some for Andrew, too. She said we had to let him eat with us. That was okay, until Andrew started to cry. I did not want crying interrupting my friends and me and our hot chocolate.

"Andrew? What is the matter?" asked Mommy.

"I left my blue sneakers at Daddy's, and I *need* them!" he wailed.

"Why?" I asked.

"Because all the boys in my class decided we would wear blue sneakers tomorrow, but I forgot mine are at Daddy's." (Andrew goes to preschool. His teacher's name is

5

Miss Jewel. Isn't that wonderful?)

Mommy sighed. Then she said, "All right. I suppose we can pick them up this afternoon. Hannie, why don't I drive you home today? That way your mother will not have to come over here, and Andrew can run across the street and get his shoes."

Mommy thought that was a good answer to the problem, but all I could think was, "Darn it. Boo and bullfrogs."

Karen and Andrew

Why was I mad? I was mad because suddenly our afternoon was over. We had to drive Hannie home, and all because Andrew is a two-two. I guess that does not make much sense to you. To understand about two-twos you have to understand about my two families. I better begin at the beginning.

A long time ago, when I was just a little kid, Andrew and I had one family: Mommy, Daddy, Andrew, me. We lived together in a big house. (It was the house

7

Daddy had grown up in.) I thought we were happy, but I found out that Mommy and Daddy were not. They began to fight. Not a little, a lot. Finally they said they did not want to live together anymore. They loved Andrew and me very much, but they did not love each other.

So they got a divorce. Mommy moved into a little house next door to Nancy, and Daddy stayed in the big house across from Hannie. After awhile, Mommy and Daddy decided to get married again, but not to each other. Mommy married Seth. That is how he became my stepfather. And Daddy married Elizabeth, my stepmother. And now Andrew and I have two families.

In my little-house family are Mommy, Seth, Andrew, me, Rocky, Midgie, Emily Junior, and Bob. Rocky and Midgie are Seth's cat and dog. Emily Junior is my pet rat. And Bob is Andrew's hermit crab.

In my big-house family are Daddy, Elizabeth, Andrew, me, Kristy, Sam, Charlie,

David Michael, Emily Michelle, Nannie, Shannon, Boo-Boo, Crystal Light the Second, Goldfishie, Emily Junior, and Bob. (Emily Junior and Bob go back and forth with Andrew and me.) Isn't that a big family? A big family for a big house.

Kristy, Sam, Charlie, and David Michael are Elizabeth's kids. (She was married once before she married Daddy.) So they are my stepsister and stepbrothers. Kristy is thirteen and a very good baby-sitter. I love her. (I always wanted a big sister.) Sam and Charlie are even older. They go to high school. David Michael is seven like me, but he does not go to Stoneybrook Academy. Emily Michelle is my little sister. She is two and a half. Daddy and Elizabeth adopted her from the faraway country of Vietnam. (I named my special rat after her.) Nannie is Elizabeth's mother. That makes her my stepgrandmother. She helps out with the house and all the kids. Shannon is David Michael's big floppy puppy. Boo-

Boo is Daddy's fat old cat. And Crystal Light and Goldfishie are both (what else?) goldfish.

Okay. Now I will tell you why Andrew is a two-two. And why I am a two-two, too. It is because we have two of so many things. Andrew and I have two houses and two families, two mommies and two daddies, two cats and two dogs. We have clothes and books and toys at the big house. And other clothes and books and toys at the little house. I have two bicycles, one at each house. And Andrew has two trikes, I have two stuffed kitty-cats that look just the same. Moosie stays at the big house, Goosie stays at the little house. Of course, I have my two best friends, Hannie and Nancy. I even have two pairs of glasses. The blue pair is for reading. The pink pair is for the rest of the time. So I am Karen Two-Two and my brother is Andrew Two-Two. (I thought up our names after Ms. Colman read a book to my class. It was called *Jacob Two-Two Meets the Hooded Fang*.)

You would think that, as two-twos, Andrew and I would have everything we need, no matter which house we are staying at. But that is not always true. Every now and then we leave something behind. Such as Andrew's blue sneakers. And then we have a little problem. I will tell you a secret, though. *Most* of the time, I feel extra, extra special — because I have *two* families to love, and two families who love me back. I guess I am glad to be Karen Two-Two.

3

The Candy Contest

"Hootie! Come here, Hootie," I called.

I bent over and peered into Hootie's cage. Hootie is our class guinea pig.

"Karen, what are you doing?" asked Hannie, as she ran into our room.

"I brought a carrot for Hootie," I replied.

It was a Monday morning. My classmates were starting to arrive at school. We gathered in Ms. Colman's room. Hannie and Nancy and I sat on some desks in the back. We tried to hold a private conversation, but we could not. Pamela Harding kept bothering us. Pamela is my best enemy, and Jannie and Leslie, her friends, are my enemies, too.

I jumped to the floor. "Pamela Harding," I yelled, "you — "

"Indoor voice, Karen," said Ms. Colman. Our teacher was hurrying into the room. She looked very busy. My classmates and I ran to our desks.

" 'Bye!" I called to Hannie and Nancy.

"See you later," they replied.

Hannie and Nancy get to sit in the back row of our room. I have to sit in the front row. That is because I wear glasses. The other glasses-wearers in my class are Ms. Colman, Natalie Springer, and Ricky Torres. I sit between Natalie and Ricky. Guess what. Ricky is my pretend husband. We got married on the playground one day.

"Okay, girls and boys," said Ms. Colman. "I would like to make two announcements. Settle down, please."

Oh, goody. Ms. Colman was going to

make two of her Surprising Announcements.

"Class," began our teacher, "as you know, Halloween is just a few weeks away. That means our school Halloween parade is just a few weeks away, too. And soon our class will begin a special parade project. During October, each of you will work with a kindergartener in Mr. Posner's room. You will help him or her make a costume to wear in the parade."

Well, that sounded like fun. I wondered who my kindergartener would be. Then I thought about our school parade. It is fun, too. On Halloween, all the students at Stoneybrook Academy bring their costumes to school. In the afternoon, we wear them to the auditorium. Then each class parades before the other classes. And three kids in each class win prizes for their costumes.

". . . so get ready to work with your kindergarten friends," Ms. Colman was saying. She paused. Then she went on. "I want to mention another Halloween project

14

to you. Some of you may remember that last summer a library in Stamford burned down. Now people are raising money to build a new library and to buy books for it. If you like, you could help raise some money for the library, too. Polly's Fine Candy has started a candy-selling project. If you go to Polly's, you can find out how to sell bags of little candy bars door-to-door. The candy bars are perfect for trick-or-treaters, so lots of people will want to buy them. The money you collect will be given to the library. If you are interested in selling candy, talk to your parents and ask them to take you to Polly's Fine Candy.''

I turned around and looked at Nancy and Hannie in the back of the room. We grinned at each other.

"Oh," said Ms. Colman, "I almost forgot. The person who sells the most bags of candy will win a gift certificate at Polly's.''

Cool. Free candy from the best candy store in town!

At recess, Nancy and Hannie and I met

by the swings for a private talk.

"Do you guys want to sell candy?" I asked them.

They nodded. We all wanted to help the library. We decided that if one of us won the gift certificate, she would share it with the others.

Polly's Fine Candy

After school that day, Hannie rode home on the bus with Nancy and me. When we reached my house, we were excited. We were jumping around.

"Mommy, can we sell candy to help the library?" I asked her.

"Could you take us to Polly's Fine Candy?" asked Nancy.

It took a little while, but finally I explained to Mommy about the candy-selling project. Then Mommy talked to Mrs. Papadakis and Mrs. Dawes. Soon we were

17

downtown, and Mommy was looking for a parking space near Polly's. When she found one, my friends and I rushed out of the car. Andrew followed us.

"Look! Look!" I cried. In the window of Polly's Fine Candy was a haunted house. It was made from hundreds and hundreds of candy corns.

"There is a candy witch!" exclaimed Andrew.

"And a candy jack-o'-lantern," said Nancy.

"And a candy monster," said Hannie.

See why we like Polly's Fine Candy so much?

Mommy led us inside the store. We stood for a moment and looked at the rows and rows of candy jars.

"May I help you?" asked a woman behind the counter.

"We are here because we want to sell candy to help the library," I told her importantly. "My friends and I. Our teacher told us about it today."

18

"Oh," said the woman. "Good for you." She smiled at us. "Come over here and I will show you what to do."

The woman took us to a table covered with forms and order pads. "Selling the candy is easy," she began. "For one thing, you do not have to lug around a big box of candy. Just take this sample bag with you. Then ask people how many bags they'd like to buy, and write down the order. Write it down here, on this form. After that, collect the money for the candy and put it in this envelope. The candy will be delivered the week before Halloween. Isn't that easy?"

It sounded very easy. So Hannie and Nancy and I each took an envelope, a pad of forms, and a bag of candy. We were ready to become door-to-door sales-people.

We left Polly's. Andrew was whining. "But I *want* candy corn," he wailed.

"Not now," said Mommy firmly. "And please stop whining."

Andrew did not stop whining until I cried, "Oh, look! Happy Halloween!"

Happy Halloween is a store in Stoneybrook that opens every year just for the month of October. It sells masks and costumes and fake noses and rubber hands and plastic spiderwebs and all sorts of cool things.

"Please could we go inside?" I asked. "Puh-*lease*? Maybe we will get some ideas for our costumes."

Nancy and Hannie and Andrew and I planned to make our costumes. We hardly ever buy them. So we did not want to get anything at Happy Halloween. We just wanted to look around.

Mommy said we could run inside.

"Hey!" said Hannie. "Here is a puppy costume!"

"Here is a monster's eyeball," said Nancy.

"Here is fake blood," said Andrew.

"Look at this costume. It is . . . it is a telephone!" I exclaimed.

Andrew and my friends and I looked and looked. We saw lots of cool costumes. But when we left the store, we still did not know what we wanted to be for Halloween.

Karen's Bet

Hannie and Nancy and I decided that if we were going to be salespeople, we should look professional. Each of us put our envelopes and our forms and our sample candy into a bag with a handle. We wrote CANDY FOR SALE on the bags. And we decided that when we were out selling our candy we should stick pencils over our ears, and wear school clothes. School clothes would look more grown-up than blue jeans and play clothes.

"We can sell our candy in lots of places," said Nancy.

"Yup. The little-house neighborhood *and* the big-house neighborhood," I added. "We know so many people."

It was the next morning. My friends and I were in our classroom again, waiting for school to begin. We were talking about how and where we could sell the bags of candy.

"Mommy and Daddy said we can only go to houses if we know the people who live in them. We cannot go to strangers' houses," said Nancy.

"My mommy and daddy said the same thing," agreed Hannie.

"Mine, too." I nodded. "But that is okay. And you know what else? If Kristy or a grown-up comes with us, maybe we could sell candy downtown — to the people who work in stores."

"Hey! Or at our parents' offices!" exclaimed Hannie.

My friends and I had lots of good ideas. We were so busy talking that we did not notice Pamela and Jannie and Leslie for a long time. When I did glance up, I whispered loudly, "Oh, no! Look!"

Nancy and Hannie looked where I was pointing. There were our enemies. They were crowded around Pamela's desk. And they were looking at forms and envelopes. The forms and envelopes were from Polly's Fine Candy.

"They are going to sell candy, too!" cried Nancy.

"Shhh!" I hissed. But I was too late. Pamela had heard her. She looked back at us.

"Are *you* selling candy?" she asked.

"Yes. Are you?" (Pamela nodded.) "Where?" I asked.

"Why do you care?" replied Pamela.

I thought for a moment. "I guess I do not care — since we are going to sell more candy than you are."

"Who says?"

"I say."

"Oh, yeah? You are not going to sell more. We are," said Pamela. "In fact, Jannie and Leslie and I are going to win that gift certificate."

"Oh, no you are not. *We* are going to win it."

"No way."

"Want to bet?" I asked.

"Sure," said Pamela. "What do you want to bet?"

"Nothing. Gentleman's bet. Just for fun."

"Ha! That means you are afraid you will lose."

"It does not!" I cried.

"Does too. But so what? I do not care, as long as we win."

"The Three Musketeers are going to beat you!" exclaimed Hannie suddenly.

Pamela shrugged. "Whatever."

"Come on, you guys," I said to my friends. I pulled them into a corner of the room. "We can beat them. I know it."

"Right," agreed Nancy. "We just have to do all the things we were talking about. We will sell to everybody. To people in stores. To *everybody*."

"One for all and all for one?" I said.

Hannie and Nancy and I clasped hands. The bet was on.

Leah

"Okay, people. Line up at the door, please," said Ms. Colman that afternoon. "It is time to go to Mr. Posner's room and meet the kindergarteners."

Ms. Colman led my classmates and me down the hall. We passed one of the kindergarten classrooms. Then we stopped at Mr. Posner's door. Ms. Colman knocked on it. She waved through the window.

Mr. Posner opened the door and let us inside. "Welcome," he said.

I looked around. The kindergarten room

sure was different from our second-grade room. There were no desks, just two long tables. Around the room I saw blocks and toys and easels and dolls, as well as books and writing paper and some math games. On one of the tables was a cage with two mice inside. On the outside of the cage was a sign: *Hunca Munca and Stuart Little*. I decided I liked Mr. Posner's room.

"Hello, boys and girls," said Mr. Posner to my classmates and me. "Find a seat on the floor. Let me tell you about our project. Each one of you will be paired with one of my students. Together you will make a costume for your new kindergarten friend to wear in the Halloween parade. Over there are the things you can use to make the costumes." Mr. Posner pointed to several big boxes. Spilling out of the boxes were feathers and buttons and old clothes and scraps of fabric and more. We would be able to make terrific costumes with those things, I thought.

"Now," Mr. Posner continued, "let me

tell you who your partners will be." He started calling out names. After he called my name, he said, "Leah Frenning," and a little girl with two long braids down her back stood up shyly.

Later, Mr. Posner said we could work wherever we wanted to. So Leah and I sat down on the rug in the story corner. I smiled at Leah. "I am Karen," I reminded her. "I am seven. How old are you?"

"Five," she replied.

"I have a little brother. He is almost five," I said. "He loves Halloween, but he does not know what he wants to be this year. Do you know what you want to be?"

Leah frowned. "Mmm . . . maybe a . . . no . . . maybe . . . I do not know."

"That's okay. I will suggest some things. How about a princess?" Leah shook her head. "A witch? No? Okay, how about a ghost? A cat? A monster?"

Leah kept shaking her head. "Maybe a . . . no," she said.

30

"An angel? A fairy? A doctor? A race-car driver?"

"No. I am thinking of the little things in the woods. . . . An elf! That's it. I want to be an elf," said Leah. "I mean, I think I do."

"All right. Let's look at the stuff in the boxes." Helping Leah was going to be easy, I thought. After all, she was about Andrew's age, and I am good with my brother. Plus, an elf costume should be easy to make. We would just need some green felt.

"And some green feathers and buttons," I said to Leah. "Also, do you have a green leotard at home? That would be good."

"Yes," replied Leah. "But maybe, um, maybe I do not want to bring it in."

"What do you mean? Why?" I asked.

Leah looked at the floor. She whispered something.

"What?" I could not hear her.

"Maybe I do not want to be in the parade," she said more loudly.

"You don't want to be in the parade? Why not?"

"I do not want all those people looking at me."

Hmm. I just love to have people looking at me. But not everyone feels that way. "Does this mean you do not want to work on the costume?" I asked.

Leah shrugged.

Uh-oh. I had not expected this problem.

The Milky Ways

That afternoon, the Three Musketeers became candy-sellers. We rode the school bus to the little house. We brushed our hair and tidied ourselves up and picked up our candy bags.

Mommy *almost* did not let us out the door.

"I think a grown-up should go with you," she said.

"Oh, no! *Please* let us go by ourselves," I cried. "We *promise* we will only visit people we know. If we do not know who lives in a house then we will not ring the door-bell. Honest."

"We-ell . . . all right," said Mommy.

"Yes!" shouted the Three Musketeers.

We ran outside with our bags. Then we slowed down. We walked to Nancy's door. Nancy rang her own bell. Mrs. Dawes answered it. She was carrying Danny. "Hello," she said.

"Hello," replied Nancy. "Mommy, I mean, madame, we are selling candy to help build a new library in Stamford. Would you like to buy a bag?"

"Or a few bags?" I interrupted.

"Yes, or a few bags?" said Nancy. "Each bag has twenty little candy bars inside. Perfect for trick-or-treaters."

"That *is* perfect," agreed Mrs. Dawes. "I will take three bags."

"Cool!" exclaimed Hannie. "I mean, thank you very much, madame. That will be seven dollars and fifty cents." (Hannie is very good at math. It is her best subject.)

Hannie and Nancy and I grinned at each other. Then Nancy said, "Okay, now I just need to fill out this form. Half of it will be your receipt."

"And you pay us now, madame," I said. "Then the candy will be delivered to you the week before Halloween."

Nancy handed Mrs. Dawes her receipt, and Mrs. Dawes handed her the money. Nancy put it in her envelope.

"Okay, now where should we go?" asked Hannie as we left Nancy's house.

"Over to Willie and Kathryn's," I said.

We dashed across the street. I rang the bell. Kathryn's daddy answered it. And he bought two bags of candy from me.

"This is easy," I said as we ran to the sidewalk. "Okay, Hannie. The next house is yours."

We worked our way down the street. We stopped in at almost every house. And each person bought at least one bag of candy. Then we headed toward Bobby Gianelli's house. Bobby is in Ms. Colman's class, too.

We used to think he was a bully, but he is really not so bad.

"We are going to beat the pants off Pamela," I said. "Come on, you guys. Here is Bobby's house. And it's my turn to sell."

But you will never guess what we saw at Bobby's. Pamela, Leslie, and Jannie. And they had just sold candy to Mrs. Gianelli.

My mouth dropped open.

Nancy and Hannie and I stood on the sidewalk. We waited for Pamela, Leslie, and Jannie to see us. When they did, Pamela called, "Hello, Three Musketeers!"

"What are you doing over here in my neighborhood?" I replied. "You do not live around here."

"We are just doing our job," said Pamela.

"Just raising money for the library," added Leslie.

"Well, do it somewhere else," I said.

"Yeah, stay in your own neighborhood," said Nancy.

"We do not have to," said Jannie. "There is no law about where we can go."

"Yeah. You guys think you are so great," said Pamela. "Just because you have a name for yourselves. But get this — we have a name, too. We are the Milky Ways."

Well, for heaven's sake.

The Little Engine
That Could

The Three Musketeers did not know what to think about the Milky Ways. All we wanted to do that afternoon was get away from them. So we walked back to my house. We flopped onto the front stoop.

"I cannot believe it," said Nancy.

"The Milky Ways are gigundo pests," added Hannie.

"At least we sold a lot of candy," I said. "Let's count up."

We had sold eighteen bags altogether. Then we counted our money.

"Forty-five dollars!" exclaimed Hannie. "Cool!"

I told myself to think about the forty-five dollars for the library, and not about the pesty Milky Ways.

That night, Andrew and I poked through our box of dress-up clothes.

"We better decide on our Halloween costumes," I said to my brother. "We need to get to work on them, if we want to finish them in time."

"Are you going to be a witch again?" Andrew asked me.

I shook my head. "Nope. I want to be something different this year, something really good. Something better than Pamela."

"Better than Pamela?"

"Yes. I want to beat her in the Halloween parade. I am going to win a prize. And I do *not* want Pamela to win one. So I need a great costume."

Andrew pulled a hard hat out of the box. "You could be a construction worker."

I shook my head. "No."

"A pilot? A cowgirl?"

"No."

"Well, I know what I want to be."

"You do?" said Mommy. She poked her head in the doorway.

"Yup. I want to be the Little Engine That Could. I mean, I want to be the train." Andrew looked quite pleased with himself.

"A whole train?" repeated Mommy. She rubbed her eyes. "Hmm. Maybe we will need a little help with your costumes this year. Would you like me to find out if Kristy could come over a few afternoons and give us a hand?"

"Yes!" Andrew and I cried. "Yes, yes, yes!"

Then we waited by the phone while Mommy called Kristy. Kristy said she would be happy to help us. Now if I could just think of a good costume. . . .

Karen's Promise

Halloween was coming soon, and I did not have an idea for my costume. But Leah's elf costume was coming along nicely.

Even though she said she was not going to wear it.

One afternoon my classmates and I were in Mr. Posner's room again. We were working away with our kindergarten partners.

"You are going to be the best elf in the parade," I said to Leah.

I was kneeling on the floor. Leah stood

before me. She was dressed in green from her head to her toes. "No I am not," she replied. "I do not want to wear it." She paused. "And I mean it. I am not even going to finish it."

"But you have to wear it. And you especially have to finish it. I do not want Ms. Colman to think I was not helping you."

"Karen, I do not want everyone looking at me."

"How about if you finish your costume, but when you march in the parade you wear your regular clothes?"

"Then everyone will look at me because I will be the only person who is *not* wearing a costume." Leah's lip trembled.

I sighed. "Are you going to finish your costume?"

Leah shook her head slowly.

I did not know what to do. I stood up. And when I did, Pamela brushed by me. "I sold eight more bags yesterday," she whispered.

"So?" I replied.

"So we are going to beat you," she said in a singsong voice.

I stuck my tongue out at her. Pamela turned her back and walked away.

"What is that girl's name?" Leah asked me.

"Meanie-mo," I muttered.

Leah nodded. "That is what I would call her, too," she said.

I grinned at Leah. I liked her. I liked her even if she *was* stubborn. And then I had an idea. "Leah," I said, "are you going trick-or-treating this year?"

"Of course," replied Leah.

"And what are you going to wear when you go trick-or-treating?"

Leah frowned. "I guess . . . my elf costume?"

"Okay. Then we better finish it, even if you do not want to march in the parade. Right? You still need a good costume."

Leah sighed. "Okay."

"Great. Now let's decide how to decorate your hat."

Leah and I began to search through a box of yarn and scraps and buttons. Suddenly I saw an enormous green button. "Perfect!" I cried. I reached for it — and another hand snatched it away.

"Sorry," said Jannie. "I saw it first." She dashed away with the button.

"Is her name Meanie-mo, too?" asked Leah.

"It ought to be. Come on, let's look in that other box." I took Leah by the hand. And that was when I got a great idea. "Leah," I said, "you stay here and look for green things. I have to talk to Mr. Posner and Ms. Colman for a minute. I will be right back."

The teachers were standing by Mr. Posner's desk. I told them about Leah. I said she had decided not to walk in the parade.

"Leah is very shy," said Mr. Posner.

"But I have an idea," I told him. "I bet Leah would walk in the parade if I walked with her. I could hold her hand. Then she would not feel so scared. Could I do that?"

Mr. Posner and Ms. Colman looked at each other. Then they smiled. "Of course," replied Mr. Posner. "That is a very good idea."

I ran back to Leah. I told her I would hold her hand. "*Then* would you be in the parade?" I asked her.

"Yes," Leah said seriously. "Thank you, Karen."

Too Late

One afternoon I was sitting on the floor in our playroom. I was looking through the box of dress-up clothes again. I was still trying to decide on a Halloween costume. I had just found a big fuzzy hat when I heard the phone ring. Andrew answered it. He just loves to answer the phone. It makes him feel grown-up.

"Who should I say is calling?" I heard him say importantly. Then he yelled, "Karen! It's Nancy!"

I ran into the kitchen. "Thanks, Andrew," I said. I took the phone from him. "Hi, Nancy!"

"Hi! I just had a great idea. Tomorrow you and Hannie and I could bring our candy-selling stuff to school. We could sell candy to all the teachers. I bet we would sell tons of bags."

"Nancy, that *is* a great idea. Let's try to get to school early."

"Definitely," agreed Nancy. "Maybe someone will drive us so we do not have to wait for the bus. I will call Hannie now to tell her the idea."

"Okay. And let's dress up tomorrow," I said.

The next day, Hannie and Nancy and I remembered our bags. And we dressed up in extra-nice school clothes. We had just one little problem. No one could drive us to school. We had to wait for our buses after all. So we did not arrive at school early.

"Oh, well," said Nancy when we met in

our classroom. "We still have time to sell a little candy."

We gathered up our things. We walked primly out of our classroom.

"Where should we go first?" asked Hannie.

"To Mr. Posner's room," I replied. "Then we will work our way through the school. First-grade rooms, second-grade rooms, all the way to the big kids' classrooms. Is that a good plan?"

"Yes," replied Hannie and Nancy.

And then we saw Pamela, Leslie, and Jannie. They were leaving Mr. Posner's room. They were holding their candy receipts. And they were stuffing some money into one of their envelopes.

"Hi, Three Musketeers," said Leslie.

Jannie eyed our CANDY FOR SALE bags. "You were not going to sell candy to the teachers, were you?" she asked.

"Yes we were!" I cried.

"Sorry. Too late," said Pamela. "You

should have gotten here early, like we did.
We have visited every teacher in the school
already."

"But . . . but . . . NO FAIR!" I shouted.

"Sorry," said Pamela again.

That afternoon my friends and I took our
candy-selling bags and walked down my
street. We walked past Bobby's house.
Then we kept going until we were in . . .
Pamela's neighborhood.

"But we do not know anybody here,"
said Nancy.

"Yes, we do. We know a few people," I
said. "This is Molly Foley's house. Come
on."

We had not even reached Molly's front
door when I heard someone shout, "Hey!
What are *you* doing over here?"

My friends and I turned around. There
were the Milky Ways.

"Just doing our job. Just selling a little
candy," I said.

"But we were going to go to Molly's house today," exclaimed Leslie.

"Sorry," I replied. "Too late."

"Yeah, too late!" called Hannie and Nancy.

Then the Three Musketeers stuck out their tongues at the Milky Ways.

The Wild Thing

"Kristy is here! Kristy is here!" called Andrew. He ran to the front door.

I was right behind him. Together we flung the door open. We were ready to work on our Halloween costumes.

I had just one little problem. I still did not know what I wanted to be.

Andrew and I jumped all over Kristy.

"Can you make me into a train?" asked Andrew.

"Can you help me decide on a costume?" I asked.

Mommy smiled at us. "They are all yours, Kristy," she said. "Good luck."

Andrew and I led Kristy into the playroom.

"Okay," said Kristy. "First, Andrew, can you bring me *The Little Engine That Could*? And now, Karen, let's think about your costume. You know, Andrew had a very good idea. He decided to be a character in a book he likes. Maybe you could do that, too."

That *was* a good idea. "Hmm. I could be Paddington Bear," I said. "Or Charlotte the spider or Willy Wonka or the Cat in the Hat."

"Or Doctor Dolittle or Clifford the Big Red Dog," added Kristy.

"Or — or, wait! I know!" I cried. "I've got it! I will be a Wild Thing from *Where the Wild Things Are*. That will be a great costume!"

"Terrific," agreed Kristy.

"I bet it will be the best in the class,"

I went on. "I bet it will be better than Pamela's."

Kristy eyed me, but she did not say anything.

Andrew returned with his book then, and I went looking for *Where the Wild Things Are*. When I had found it, Andrew and Kristy and I turned the pages of the books.

"You guys do not choose easy costumes, do you?" said Kristy.

"No, but we choose fun ones," I replied.

Kristy grinned. "I guess that is true. Now, let's see. Andrew, how can we turn you into a train?"

"Maybe with cardboard boxes," said Andrew.

"Yeah, we could attach a train of them behind him, and then Andrew could wear one big one around his middle, and that would be the engine!" I exclaimed. "And for me . . . hmm. How are we going to

make me look furry? And I will need horns, I think."

Andrew and I could not wait to begin working on our costumes.

The Fight

One morning Nancy and I were riding the bus to school when Nancy leaned over and whispered something in my ear. "I am a little afraid of Pamela," she said. She looked embarrassed.

"You are?" I replied.

"Yes. And Hannie is too. Pamela is always so mean to us now. So are Jannie and Leslie, but Pamela is the meanest."

This was not a good thing. I thought about it in the morning when I saw Pamela turn around in her seat and make mean faces at Nancy and Hannie. I thought about it in the cafeteria when Pamela pushed in front of Nancy on the lunch line. And I thought about it on the playground while the Milky Ways hogged the swings.

"*I* want to swing today, too," said Hannie.

"Tell Pamela she has to give you a turn," I said.

"Noooo, I don't want to," said Hannie.

"It will be okay. Just tell her," I said patiently.

"Pamela!" called Hannie. "I would like a turn now, please!"

"You will have to wai-ait!" Pamela called back in her singsong voice.

Hannie scuffed her feet. My friends and I waited for ten minutes. Then I nudged Hannie and said, "Tell her again."

"No," said Hannie. "No way."

"Want me to try?" offered Nancy. Before Hannie could answer, Nancy was shouting, "Pamela, could you please give Han — "

"You will have to wai-ait!" called Pamela again. And the Milky Ways began to laugh.

That did it. I ran to the swings. I stood in front of Pamela so that when she swung forward she almost touched me. "Get off of the swings!" I cried. "You cannot hog them all day. Get off."

"Make me."

I moved closer to Pamela's swing. The next time she swung forward, I caught her feet. And I stopped her. But Pamela would not get off the swing.

By now, a bunch of kids from our class were watching us. Bobby and Ricky and the boys had stopped their game of kickball. Natalie was standing with Hannie and Nancy. And Leslie and Jannie had stopped swinging and were watching us, too.

"Make me," said Pamela again.

So I slugged Pamela in the face.

I had not known I was going to do that. I had not *meant* to do it. But suddenly I was gasping, and Pamela was gasping, and her cheek was turning bright red.

For a moment, everyone else was quiet. Then the other kids started to talk. I could hear them say things like, "Karen *hit* her!" and "Did you see that?" I even heard one person (I do not know who) say, "Someone finally hit Pamela." Then someone else said, "That is wrong. Hitting is not the way to solve problems. Everyone knows that."

I knew I should apologize to Pamela then. I had hurt her and I had embarrassed her. But I just could not tell her I was sorry. She had been too mean to my friends and me lately.

Finally Leslie said, "Pamela, are you all right?"

"Of course I am," replied Pamela. She jumped to her feet. "Come on, you guys. Let's get out of here."

The Milky Ways ran off. I stared after them. Then I looked for Hannie and Nancy. I did not see Pamela again until it was time to line up and wait to be let inside. Pamela got on line with everyone else. She would not look at me.

The Boys Tattle

My classmates and I did not say anything about Pamela while we waited in line. In fact, we did not say anything at all. We stood silently in our places. Then we walked silently into school and along the hallway. We walked silently into our classroom. Ms. Colman looked up from her desk as we silently took our places.

She knew something was wrong.

"Boys and girls?" she said.

Nobody answered her.

And then she saw Pamela's face. She saw

her cheek, which was bright red where I had hit her. "Pamela!" she exclaimed. "What happened to you?"

Pamela shrugged. "Nothing."

We were all watching Pamela, every single one of us kids. We were waiting for her to say what I had done. We were waiting for her to tattle.

"Pamela?" said Ms. Coleman again. "Somebody hit you. I want you to tell me what happened. What was the fight about?"

"Nothing," Pamela repeated. She would not look at Ms. Colman.

Ms. Colman looked at her, though. She looked at her hard. Then she looked around at the rest of us.

"All right," said our teacher. She sounded very stern. Ms. Colman hardly ever sounds stern, so I knew she was serious. "I want someone to tell me what went on out there on the playground."

My classmates and I stopped looking at

Pamela. But we could not look at Ms. Colman, either. We stared at our hands, or the floor, or the blackboard, or out the windows.

Nobody said a word.

"I think every one of you knows what happened," Ms. Colman went on. "And I would like somebody to tell me about it. Fighting is serious. Hitting is very serious. Any kind of hurting is very serious. It is not the way to solve problems."

"That is what I said!" cried Natalie Springer. And then she clapped her hand over her mouth. "Oops," she muttered.

So Natalie had said that. I knew she was right. But somehow that made me angry now. I narrowed my eyes at her. Dumb old Natalie with her lisp, and her socks that are always falling down.

I hoped Ms. Colman had finished speaking. But she had not. And what she said next surprised me. "All right, boys and girls," she continued. "I must tell you something. I am having a problem. My problem is that I need to know who hit Pamela and why. I need somebody to tell me what happened. But none of you wants to talk about it. So I am going to solve my problem by saying that until someone tells me the truth, none of you may go outside for recess. Starting tomorrow, we will spend our recesses indoors, sitting quietly at our desks. Now please take out your autumn leaf projects."

I could not believe it! No outdoor recess until somebody snitched on me?

After school that day, Nancy said to me, "Karen, what are you going to *do*?" She looked worried.

"I don't know. I do not want everyone to miss recess. But I cannot tell Ms. Colman I hit Pamela." I paused. "Do you think anyone else will tell on me? Pamela won't talk. She is too embarrassed."

"Nobody wants to tattle," replied Nancy.

Nancy was wrong. The next day, nobody tattled all morning. Even when Ms. Colman said, "Who will tell me what happened?"

But at noon she said, "All right. After lunch, please return to our room for recess." And then all the boys in the room stood up. Together they said, "Karen Brewer did it."

The Principal's Office

I glared at the boys. I made evil eyes at them. They were such babies. Just because they wanted to play outside, they had to go tattle. Every one of them. Even Ricky, my pretend husband. He should have known better than to tell on his wife. But he had gone along with the other boys.

"Karen? Pamela?" said Ms. Colman. "Is this true?"

I glanced over my shoulder at Pamela. Then we nodded. "Yes," I said.

"Very well. Boys and girls, you may go

69

to the cafeteria for lunch. Afterward, you may go outside for recess. Except for Karen and Pamela. You stay here."

Pamela and I stood at Ms. Colman's desk. The other kids hurried into the hallway. Hannie and Nancy looked at me sadly on their way out.

"Now," Ms. Colman said to Pamela and me, "I want to hear the story from both of you. Pamela, you go first."

"Um," Pamela began, "well, Karen was bothering me on the swings and then she just hit me."

Ms. Colman looked doubtful. "Karen?"

"Pamela was being mean to Nancy and Hannie and me. She has been mean for a long time. And yesterday she would not let Hannie have a turn on the swings, even when Hannie asked nicely. So, um, I hit her."

Ms. Colman set her mouth in a firm line. "I am not happy with either one of you," she said. "And I am surprised at you. Pamela, you know that in this school you are expected to share. We talk about that a lot."

"Pamela is a swing hog," I spoke up.

"And Karen, I would never have expected you to hit someone," Ms. Colman continued. "Both of you will have to go to the principal's office."

The *principal's* office? But that meant we had done something very, very serious.

"Did you girls bring your lunches today?" asked Ms. Colman.

"Yes," we said.

"Okay. Get them from your cubbies. You may eat them while you wait to see Mrs. Titus. Come along."

Ms. Colman led Pamela and me down the hall to the office. I have been to see our vice-principal, but never the principal herself. Pamela and I sat on a bench outside the office. We tried to eat our lunches while Ms. Colman talked to Mrs. Titus. After awhile, Ms. Colman left. "I will see you in class later, girls," she said.

Then Mrs. Titus called us inside. Pamela and I threw away our lunch bags. We sat in chairs facing Mrs. Titus at her desk.

"I hear you had a fight," said Mrs. Titus. "Will you please tell me about it?"

Pamela and I told our stories again. Pamela finished hers by saying, "And hitting is never right. Karen should not have done that."

"No," agreed Mrs. Titus. "She should not have. And you, Pamela, should have shared your swing. Both of you have a lot to learn about manners, about courtesy, and about working out disagreements. And you need to remember that rules must be followed all the time, not just when you feel like following them. Your behavior yesterday was not what I expect from students at Stoneybrook Academy. I am not pleased. So you will have to be punished."

"What is our punishment?" asked Pamela in a small voice.

"Neither one of you may be in the Halloween parade," replied Mrs. Titus. "I will call your parents to tell them about my decision."

"We can't be in the parade?" I cried. But then how could I beat Pamela by winning a prize? And how could I show off the wonderful furry costume Kristy and I were making? I could not. Boo and bullfrogs.

That night, Mommy and Seth had A TALK with me. They were not pleased with my behavior either. And Mommy had not been pleased with her phone call from Mrs. Titus. She said I had better remember to keep my temper. Then she said no TV for three whole nights. BOO and more bullfrogs.

Karen and Leah

Halloween was just a few days away. At the little house, Kristy had helped Andrew and me to finish our costumes. Andrew's train of cardboard boxes, and my furry suit with horns, sat in the back hallway. I would be able to wear my costume when I went trick-or-treating of course. But I could not wear it in the Halloween parade.

In school, in Mr. Posner's room, the little kids' costumes were almost finished, too. One day, Ms. Colman said to my classmates and me, "Today you must make sure the kindergarteners' costumes are ready. This is the last chance you will have to work with the kids."

That afternoon, when we arrived in Mr. Posner's room, Leah jumped up and ran to me. She was holding her costume. "Look, Karen!" she cried. "I put some more sequins on by myself. Do you like what I did?"

"It looks great," I replied. "I am glad you like it."

"I cannot wait to wear it."

"You mean when you go trick-or-treating?" I asked.

Leah nodded. Then she said, "I am kind of looking forward to the parade, too. I want everyone to see my costume. Then they will know how hard I worked. And I will not be *too* scared in the parade, since you will be with me, Karen."

Uh-oh. The parade. Mrs. Titus had said I could not be in it. But I had made a promise to Leah. I could not break my promise, either. What should I do?

I decided to talk to Ms. Colman. I talked to her at the end of the day, while my classmates were getting ready to leave school.

"Ms. Colman?" I said. I waited by her desk.

"Yes, Karen?"

"I have a problem. I need to talk to you. It is about the parade."

"Karen, you know what Mrs. Titus said. I cannot change that."

"I know. But I also promised Leah I would walk with her in the parade. I said I would hold her hand so she would not feel scared."

Ms. Colman frowned. "That is right. I had forgotten about that."

"So had I. And I do not want to break my promise to Leah."

"Hmm. Let me think about this," said Ms. Colman. "Let me talk to Mrs. Titus. See me first thing tomorrow morning."

Tomorrow? How could I wait until the next day? But I had to.

I worried about my problem all night.

The next morning I waited for Ms. Colman to enter our classroom. The moment I saw her, I ran to her. "Did you talk to Mrs. Titus?" I asked.

"Yes," replied my teacher. "And she wants to talk to you. You may go to her office right now, if you like."

Of course I wanted to talk to Mrs. Titus. So I walked to her office.

When Mrs. Titus saw me, she said, "Oh, Karen. Good morning."

"Good morning," I answered.

"Ms. Colman told me about your promise to Leah Frenning." (I nodded.) "You were very nice to make that promise. But I did tell you and Pamela that you may not be in the parade."

I nodded again. Then I said, "But I do not want to break my promise."

"No. I do not think you should do that. It would not be fair to Leah. So I have decided that you may walk with Mr. Posner's class and hold Leah's hand. But you may not wear a costume, just your school clothes. And you still may not march in the parade with your class. Do you understand?"

"Yes," I said.

Boo. I did want to show off my costume. But at least I could keep my promise to Leah.

The Sneaky Plan

I was glad that I could keep my promise to Leah. But I was mad that I could not be in the Halloween parade. I knew I should not have hit Pamela. But I still wanted everyone at Stoneybrook Academy to see my wonderful Wild Thing costume. And I still wanted to beat Pamela by winning a prize.

So I sulked around for awhile. I sulked around so much that Nancy and Hannie got tired of me. At recess the next day they played hopscotch by themselves while I sat under a tree. We were not mad. We just needed a little break from each other. At least, they said they needed a break from me.

"Boo, boo, boo," I said. I leaned against the trunk of the tree. The ground was cold under my seat. I could feel it through my coat.

Then I heard a sound. I heard someone say, "Rats, rats, ratty rats." I peered around the tree. Pamela was leaning against the other side of the trunk. She looked as sulky as I felt.

"What are *you* doing here?" she said when she saw me.

"Nothing. What are *you* doing?"

"Nothing. Where are the rest of your Musketeers?"

I shrugged. "Playing. Where are the rest of your Milky Ways?"

Pamela shrugged. "Playing."

"Anyway," I said, "thanks a lot."

"For what?" asked Pamela, frowning.

"For getting us in trouble."

"*Me*? *I* did not get us in trouble. You were the one who hit me."

"Well, I would not have hit you if you had not been so mean."

"Yeah, well . . ." Pamela paused. Finally she said, "I guess we got each other in trouble. It was not all my fault or all your fault."

"I guess," I said. "Boy, I wish you could see the costume I was going to wear in the parade. My big stepsister helped me make it. It is a Wild Thing. It even has fur and horns."

"Really?" Pamela looked interested. "Cool. I am going to be a lollipop."

"Cool!" I said. "But now no one will see us. Not at school, anyway."

"Nope. Not at school."

"I really like walking in the parade," I said. "It is one of the best things about Halloween. I always look forward to it."

"Darn old Mrs. Titus," said Pamela.

"Yeah, darn old Mrs. — " I stopped. "Hey, wait!"

"What?"

"I just had an idea. But I do not know if you would want to do it. I do not even know if we *can* do it."

"What is it?" asked Pamela.

"Well, I think I know how we can be in the parade."

"You are kidding."

"Nope. What if we had a costume that would cover us up completely, even our heads? No one would know we were wearing it."

"Because no one could see *us*," said Pamela. "But how would we sneak into the parade? How would we change into our costume?"

"Yeah. What if we got caught?" I said.

"What if our costume won a *prize*?" cried Pamela. "That would be awful! Then everyone would know what we had done."

84

"Still, don't you want to be in the parade?" I asked.

Pamela smiled. "Yes," she admitted.

"Me too," I said. "So let's do it. We will figure something out."

"Okay," agreed Pamela.

Halloween

"Hey, Andrew! It is Halloween!" I exclaimed. "Wake up!"

Andrew peered sleepily at me from under his covers. "What?" he said. And then he remembered. "Oh, yeah! Halloween!"

My brother and I ran downstairs. First we looked at our costumes again. Then we checked our trick-or-treat buckets, just to make sure they were there. Then we checked the bowl of candy bars Mommy and Seth were going to hand out that night.

I sighed. Halloween is a gigundoly wonderful holiday.

The only bad thing about it is waiting for it to happen.

I was not patient in school that day. I wiggled around a lot.

Finally, after lunch and recess, Ms. Colman said, "Okay, girls and boys. It is time to get ready for the parade."

"Yes!" I cried.

Ms. Colman looked at me oddly. I knew she was wondering why I was so excited about the parade if I was not going to be in it. So I settled down. "Now," my teacher continued, "will all the boys please take their costumes next door to Mr. Berger's room. Then Mr. Berger's girls are going to come here. You will change your clothes in the classrooms."

Pamela and I watched as the switch was made. Then we watched the girls change into their costumes. We sat at our desks as our friends turned into goblins and witches and cats and Pippi Longstocking and a teddy bear (Paddington, maybe) and a duck and a spider and lots of other things.

"Where is your costume?" a girl from Mr. Berger's room asked me.

"She can't wear it. She is being punished," said Jannie smugly.

I shot Jannie a Look. But I did not say anything. I smiled secretly at Pamela, though. Pamela and I had our daring plan. But we had not told a single person about it. Not even our very best friends.

When everyone had put on their costumes, and when their friends had helped them with their makeup and false warts and plastic scars and green rubber hands, we were ready to go to the gym. Ms. Colman and Mr. Berger led us there. They sat us on the floor behind the kindergarteners and the first-graders. Behind *us* were the third-graders, and so on. The oldest kids sat in the back.

When it was time for the parade to begin, the kindergarten teachers asked their kids to stand up. I stood up, too. It was time for me to keep my promise to Leah. I ran to her and grabbed her hand.

"Hi, Karen," she whispered. "I am glad you are here."

"Me too. You are going to be great," I told her.

The kindergarteners made a big circle in the front of the gym. Then they walked slowly around and around, so everyone could see them. Mr. Posner said to the audience, "I would like you to know that my students made their own costumes. They are very proud of them."

Leah was gripping my hand. She was not looking at the audience. But she whispered to me, "Are people staring at me, Karen?"

"They are looking at *all* of you guys," I replied. "And they are smiling. They like your costumes. I can tell."

When we had paraded around two times, Mr. Posner told us to sit down. The awards were going to be handed out. (I stayed with Leah for a few minutes.)

"First prize," said Mrs. Titus, "goes to Ari Spelling, our robot."

Everyone clapped. Mrs. Titus gave Ari a blue ribbon. Then she said, "Second prize goes to Roger Halpern."

Guess who won third prize. Leah! When Mrs. Titus gave her the yellow ribbon, Leah hugged it to herself. Then she hugged me. And I hugged her back.

The Parade

The kindergarteners sat on the floor in the gym. They wriggled. They whispered. They leaned over to look at the prizes that Leah and Roger and Ari had won. They waited for the first-graders to start marching.

While the kindergarteners wiggled and the first-graders marched, the second-graders checked their costumes and ran to Ms. Colman and Mr. Berger with questions. The gym was getting noisy.

"Come on," I whispered to Pamela. "Now is our chance."

Pamela and I looked around quickly. No one was paying attention to us. We sneaked to the door of the gym. Then we ran down the hall to our class.

"Where did you put it?" I asked Pamela.

"In my cubby." Pamela reached into her cubby and pulled out a crumpled paper grocery bag. Inside the bag was a rumpled sheet. We threw it over our heads. We were a gigantic ghost. We knew it was not a very clever costume, but these were the good things about it: 1. It covered us from our heads to our toes. No one would know we were in it. 2. We were pretty sure we would not win a prize with it.

"Did you cut out eye holes?" I asked Pamela.

"Yup. They are right here."

"But there are only two," I said.

"Well, I could not make four," Pamela replied. "Then everyone would know two people were inside." Pamela put her eyes to the holes.

"I cannot see at all!" I cried.

"I will lead us," replied Pamela.

I stood behind Pamela and put my arms around her waist. We hustled down the hallway to the gym. "What is going on?" I asked when we stopped in the doorway.

"Our class is standing up," whispered Pamela. "They are walking to the front of the gym. We will just join them as they walk by."

And that is what we did. Soon we were marching around the front of the gym. We were in the Halloween parade!

"Who is in front of us?" I asked Pamela.

"Ricky," she whispered. "Quasimodo."

"Who is behind us?"

Pamela and I tried to march and turn around together at the same time. (This was not easy.) "It is Hannie!" exclaimed Pamela.

"Does she know we are in here?"

"I don't think so."

Pamela and I followed our classmates around and around the front of the gym. Finally Pamela said, "Okay, we are going to stop now. It is time for the prizes. Sit down, Karen."

We sat while Mrs. Titus found the three prize ribbons.

"Thank you, second-graders," I heard her say a few moments later. "Your costumes are all wonderful. I am happy to award first prize to Tracy Bannon. Second prize goes to Bobby Gianelli. And third prize goes to Hank Reubens. Congratulations!"

"Okay," I said to Pamela then. "We better get out of here."

Our classmates were returning to their places in the gym. The third-graders were standing up. We had to get rid of our ghost costume fast. Before we did, though, I said, "Pamela, let's just show our friends what we did."

So Pamela grabbed Hannie, Nancy, Leslie, and Jannie as they filed by.

"Come here," she hissed. Pamela and I threw off our sheet.

"Hey!" cried Nancy. "It's you!"

Our friends were impressed. And Pamela and I were impressed with ourselves. We shook hands. Then we ditched our sheet. Nobody else ever found out what we had done.

Trick-or-treat!

"Oof! Karen, help me," said Andrew.

Andrew was standing in the living room. A cardboard box was stuck on his head. It was part of his train costume. But he did not look much like the Little Engine That Could just then.

I ran to my brother. I pulled the box down. I settled it around his middle. "Where is the rest of the train?" I asked.

Andrew pointed. "Over there. But let's wait until Kristy comes. She will help me put it on. And my makeup, too."

That was fine with me. I needed time to put on my own costume.

Ding-dong!

"There's Kristy!" I shrieked. I raced for the front door. I let my big stepsister inside.

Kristy bustled around. She attached the rest of Andrew's train to the box on his middle. She put on his makeup. Then she helped me with my makeup. Then she handed us our trick-or-treat buckets.

"Let's go get Nancy," she said.

"Wait a minute!" called Mommy. She rushed into the room with her camera. "Smile!" she said. Mommy snapped about a roll of pictures. Then she said, "Okay, go have fun. I will be here handing out candy. Seth will probably be home by the time you come back. He will want to see your costumes."

"And our full buckets," I added.

Kristy led Andrew and me next door to the Daweses' house. Nancy was waiting for us in her apple costume. That was what she had decided to be. An apple. With a worm crawling toward the stem. She had made the worm by stuffing a green sock with paper towels.

"Hello, Apple!" I called to Nancy.

"Hello, Wild Thing!" she replied. "Hi, Little Engine. Hi, Kristy."

"Hi," said Kristy. "Okay, trick-or-treaters. Let's get started."

We went to Kathryn and Willie's house first. I had forgotten that the Three Musketeers had sold candy to their father. Now I saw the bowl of little candy bars. Nancy and Andrew and I each chose one. We dropped them into our buckets. *Thunk, thunk, thunk.*

"Thank you!" we called.

We rang the bell at the house next door. "Trick-or-treat!"

Guess what. We had also sold candy there. Mr. Drucker held out a box full of the tiny candy bars. This time I chose a different kind.

We rang the bells at every house between mine and Bobby Gianelli's.

"Gosh," said Kristy at the fourth house. "This is so weird. Everyone has the exact same kind of candy."

I giggled. "Kristy," I said. "This is the candy my dad and your mom are giving out, too. The Three Musketeers sold it to them, remember?"

"Oh! This is the stuff you were selling! I forgot about that." Kristy paused. "I hope you like it," she added.

"I guess I do," I said. "Candy is candy."

"Anyway, this means we helped earn a lot of money for the library," Nancy pointed out. She tugged at her costume.

Ding-dong. Kristy rang the bell at the house next to Bobby's. A woman answered the door. "My!" she exclaimed. "Look at you three. An apple," she said to Nancy. "A Wild Thing," she said to me. "And . . . are you a train?"

Andrew beamed. "I am the Little Engine That Could. And I made the costume myself." He looked very proud.

"Wonderful," said the woman. And guess what she gave us. Big bags of Reese's Pieces. Finally — something different!

"Thank you!" called Nancy and Andrew and I as we ran toward Bobby's.

Three Thousand Dollars

Trick-or-treating was over. The Wild Thing costume and the Little Engine costume had been put away in the attic. Mommy was starting to talk about Thanksgiving. But Halloween was not *quite* over yet. That was because the winner of the candy contest had not been announced yet.

"Today is the day!" I said to Nancy and Hannie one morning at school.

"Do you think we will win?" asked Nancy.

Hannie and I shrugged. Who knew? But we would find out that afternoon. After school Mrs. Dawes was going to drive us to Polly's Fine Candy. And Polly would tell us about the contest.

That day I wiggled my way through school. Hannie and Nancy whispered their way. And Pamela, Jannie, and Leslie squirmed their way.

"Goodness, what is going on?" said Ms. Colman.

We settled down. At least for awhile. But when the bell rang, the six of us leaped out of our seats. We grabbed our things from our cubbies and raced outside.

"See you at Polly's!" I called to Pamela as we ran to our buses.

A little while later, Nancy and Hannie and I were crowding into Polly's Fine Candy. Mrs. Dawes was with us, carrying Danny. The Milky Ways were right behind us. An awful lot of people had come to Polly's to find out about the contest. The store was very noisy.

"Excuse me! Excuse me! May I have your attention, please?"

Polly was standing on a chair at the front of the crowd. She waved her arms to get our attention. Finally, the crowd quieted down.

"Thank you," said Polly. "And now, I have happy news for you. You and the other people who sold candy last month raised — are you ready for this? — over three *thousand* dollars for the library. Congratulations!"

I turned to my friends. "Three thousand dollars," I whispered. I could not believe it. Neither could Hannie and Nancy. They just looked at me, wide-eyed.

Behind us, I heard Pamela and Jannie and Leslie saying things like, "*That* much?" and "No way!" and "Three *thousand*?"

"You all worked very hard," said Polly, "and I want to thank you. I wish I could give gift certificates to each of you, but there is only one prize. And it goes to . . ." (I clutched at Hannie and Nancy) "Peggy Marino."

Someone near Polly let out a shriek. Then she made her way to Polly's chair, and Polly handed her an envelope.

"Now," continued Polly, "if you would like to see how many bags of candy each of you sold, I have posted a tally sheet next to the door. Feel free to look at it. And thank you again for your work."

Polly stepped off her chair. Nancy and Hannie and I turned around. "Come on," I said. "Let's look at the sheet. We did not win the prize. But we still might have beaten the Milky Ways."

The Three Musketeers looked at the chart. I guess *we* could have kept track of how much candy we had sold. But we had not bothered. We had been too busy with Halloween. We found our names on the chart. Then I found Pamela's name. Guess what. Pamela had sold one more bag than I had.

"Beat you," I heard Pamela say from behind me. But when I turned around, she was smiling. It was a friendly smile.

"Okay, let's figure out who sold more — the Three Musketeers or the Milky Ways," said Hannie. So we added up the numbers. And . . . we had tied.

"I don't believe it!" I cried.

"Neither do I!" said Pamela.

Then we smiled at each other again. I knew we were both thinking about sneaking into the Halloween parade. We would never forget it. It would always be our secret.

"Time to go," said Mrs. Dawes then.

My friends and I left Polly's Fine Candy. Halloween was over.

About the Author

ANN M. MARTIN lives in New York City and loves animals, especially cats. She has two cats of her own, Mouse and Rosie.

Other books by Ann M. Martin that you might enjoy are *Stage Fright*; *Me and Katie (the Pest)*; and the books in *The Baby-sitters Club* series.

Ann likes ice cream and *I Love Lucy*. And she has her own little sister, whose name is Jane.

Little Sister

Don't miss #55

KAREN'S MAGICIAN

Andrew was beaming as he walked up onto the stage. Mr. Wizard called two more people from the audience.

"Please drop your objects into the tank," said Mr. Wizard. "Then watch what happens."

Right before our eyes, the objects disappeared. But that was not all. They turned into goldfish!

"Did you see that? It was amazing!" said Andrew when he got back to his seat.

Andrew was right. Mr. Wizard's magic was truly amazing.

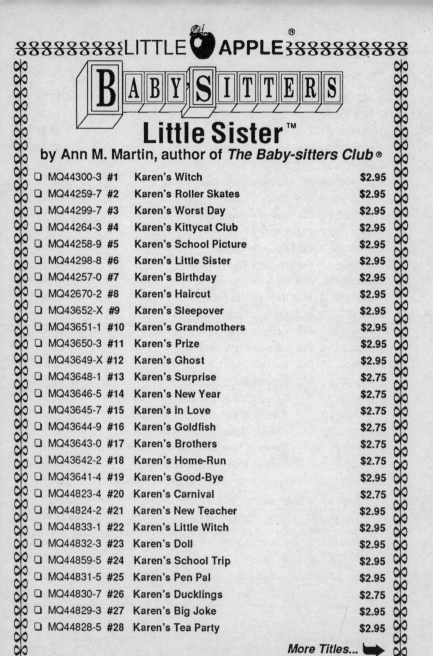

✽✽✽✽✽✽✽✽LITTLE 🍎 APPLE®✽✽✽✽✽✽✽✽

BABY·SITTERS

Little Sister™

by Ann M. Martin, author of *The Baby-sitters Club*®

❑ MQ44300-3	#1	Karen's Witch	$2.95
❑ MQ44259-7	#2	Karen's Roller Skates	$2.95
❑ MQ44299-7	#3	Karen's Worst Day	$2.95
❑ MQ44264-3	#4	Karen's Kittycat Club	$2.95
❑ MQ44258-9	#5	Karen's School Picture	$2.95
❑ MQ44298-8	#6	Karen's Little Sister	$2.95
❑ MQ44257-0	#7	Karen's Birthday	$2.95
❑ MQ42670-2	#8	Karen's Haircut	$2.95
❑ MQ43652-X	#9	Karen's Sleepover	$2.95
❑ MQ43651-1	#10	Karen's Grandmothers	$2.95
❑ MQ43650-3	#11	Karen's Prize	$2.95
❑ MQ43649-X	#12	Karen's Ghost	$2.95
❑ MQ43648-1	#13	Karen's Surprise	$2.75
❑ MQ43646-5	#14	Karen's New Year	$2.75
❑ MQ43645-7	#15	Karen's in Love	$2.75
❑ MQ43644-9	#16	Karen's Goldfish	$2.75
❑ MQ43643-0	#17	Karen's Brothers	$2.75
❑ MQ43642-2	#18	Karen's Home-Run	$2.75
❑ MQ43641-4	#19	Karen's Good-Bye	$2.95
❑ MQ44823-4	#20	Karen's Carnival	$2.75
❑ MQ44824-2	#21	Karen's New Teacher	$2.95
❑ MQ44833-1	#22	Karen's Little Witch	$2.95
❑ MQ44832-3	#23	Karen's Doll	$2.95
❑ MQ44859-5	#24	Karen's School Trip	$2.95
❑ MQ44831-5	#25	Karen's Pen Pal	$2.95
❑ MQ44830-7	#26	Karen's Ducklings	$2.75
❑ MQ44829-3	#27	Karen's Big Joke	$2.95
❑ MQ44828-5	#28	Karen's Tea Party	$2.95

More Titles... ➡

Available wherever you buy books, or use this order form.

Scholastic Inc., P.O. Box 7502, 2931 E. McCarty Street, Jefferson City, MO 65102

Please send me the books I have checked above. I am enclosing $ _____
(please add $2.00 to cover shipping and handling). Send check or money order - no cash or C.O.Ds please.

Name _____ Birthdate _____

Address _____

City _____ State/Zip _____

Please allow four to six weeks for delivery. Offer good in U.S.A. only. Sorry, mail orders are not available to residents to Canada. Prices subject to change.   BLS793

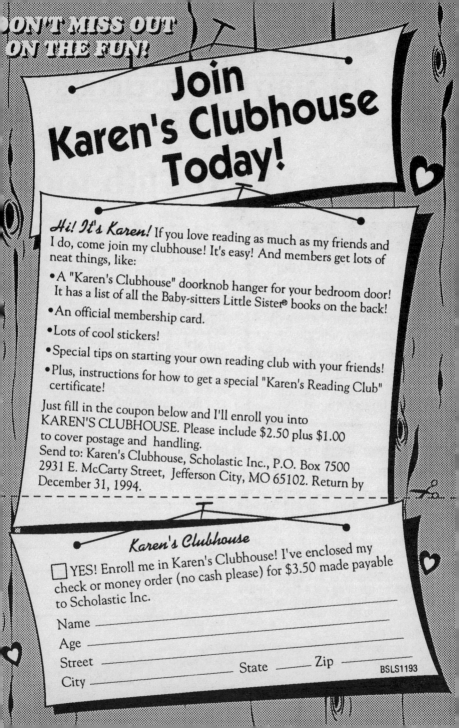

DON'T MISS OUT ON THE FUN!

Join Karen's Clubhouse Today!

Hi! It's Karen! If you love reading as much as my friends and I do, come join my clubhouse! It's easy! And members get lots of neat things, like:

- A "Karen's Clubhouse" doorknob hanger for your bedroom door! It has a list of all the Baby-sitters Little Sister® books on the back!
- An official membership card.
- Lots of cool stickers!
- Special tips on starting your own reading club with your friends!
- Plus, instructions for how to get a special "Karen's Reading Club" certificate!

Just fill in the coupon below and I'll enroll you into KAREN'S CLUBHOUSE. Please include $2.50 plus $1.00 to cover postage and handling.
Send to: Karen's Clubhouse, Scholastic Inc., P.O. Box 7500 2931 E. McCarty Street, Jefferson City, MO 65102. Return by December 31, 1994.

Karen's Clubhouse

☐ YES! Enroll me in Karen's Clubhouse! I've enclosed my check or money order (no cash please) for $3.50 made payable to Scholastic Inc.

Name —————————————————————

Age —————————————————————

Street ————————————————————

City ———————— State ——— Zip ———

BSLS1193

★ is a Video Club too!